E Off
Offen, Hilda.
As quiet as a mouse

DATE DUE			
MR 21 '96			
AP 15 '96			

Gunnison County Library
307 N. Wisconsin
Gunnison, CO 81230

S0-AJQ-471

for Karen Kennedy

Copyright © 1994 by Hilda Offen
All rights reserved.
CIP Data is available.
First published in the United States 1994 by
Dutton Children's Books,
a division of Penguin Books USA Inc.
375 Hudson Street, New York, New York 10014
Originally published in Great Britain 1994 by
Hutchinson Children's Books, an imprint of
Random House UK Limited, London
Printed in China
First American Edition
1 3 5 7 9 10 8 6 4 2
ISBN 0-525-45309-1

As Quiet as a Mouse

HILDA OFFEN

Gunnison County Library
307 N. Wisconsin
Gunnison CO 81230

Dutton Children's Books · New York

I was as quiet as a mouse,
I tiptoed all around.

Put finger to lips.
Walk on tiptoe.

I listened and listened,
but there wasn't a sound.

Put hand to ear.

Then…a gold butterfly
breathed a long sigh.

Sigh.

A worm gave a wiggle
and started to giggle.

Giggle.

"A-choo!" sneezed the hen.
Then she did it again.

Pretend to sneeze twice.

The pig was so bored
that she lay down and snored.

Snore.

"Clap your hands, girls and boys!"
said the seal. "Make a noise."

Clap your hands.

The chimp said, "I'm champ," and started to stamp.

Stamp your feet.

"You?" said the giraffe.
"Oh, don't make me laugh!"

Laugh.

The bear gave a shout,
"The wolf's here, look out!"

Shout "Look out!"

The wolf said, "I'm tough.
I'll huff and I'll puff!"

Huff and puff.

Then the dinosaur roared,
and he roared and he ROARED!

Roar.

What a terrible din!
What a noise! What a sound!

Sigh, giggle, sneeze,
snore, clap, stamp,
laugh, shout, huff
and puff, and roar.

I told them to stop!
And they all turned around.

Shout "Stop!"

I made them be quiet.
It didn't take long.

Whisper "Shhh!"

Then they danced in a circle
while I sang them a song.

Sing your favorite song.

Gunnison County Library
30?? Wisconsin
Gunnison, CO 81230